What Do You Need® to Go Camping?

PAUL ZOCH

DP Innovations

ABOUT THE AUTHOR

Paul first stumbled onto the idea for the *What Do You Need?* books while playing a game with his two children the night before leaving on a canoe trip. Their answers to his question "What do you need to go camping?" ranged from tents and flashlights to refrigerators and pianos, kindling hours of fun and eventually growing into this series. Paul lives with his family in Minnesota where he spends as much time as he can in the forest, enjoying the fresh air, wildlife, and most of all, the beautiful night sky. The only thing he enjoys more is listening to his daughter play the piano.

This book is dedicated to three special ladies in my life: my mother, Elaine; my wife, Karen; and my daughter, Mandy.

A special thanks to Christy Selbrade and Lori Sandvig.

Published by DP Innovations
53093 802nd Street Jackson, MN 56143

For ordering information or special discounts for bulk purchases, visit www.wdynbooks.com
Design and composition by Greenleaf Book Group LLC

Cover design by Greenleaf Book Group LLC
Illustrations by the creative talents at MikeMotz.com
Color by Tina Bosma from The Ad Pros

The Coleman logo and lantern shape are used with permission of The Coleman Company, Inc.
The Wall Drug name is used with permission of the Wall Drug Company

Publisher's Cataloging-In-Publication Data
(Prepared by The Donohue Group, Inc.)
Zoch, Paul.
    What do you need to go camping? / Paul Zoch ; illustrated by . . . MikeMotz.com. -- 1st ed.

    p. : col. ill. ; cm. -- (What do you need)

    Summary: Blaze and Maddy have never been camping before, and need help packing.
    ISBN: 978-0-9789484-0-5

1.   Camping--Juvenile literature. 2.   Luggage--Packing--Juvenile literature. 3. Camping. 4.   Luggage--Packing. I. MikeMotz.com. II. Title. III. Title: Camping

GV192.2 .Z63 2008
796.54   2008908012

Printed in the USA by Bang Printing, Brainerd, MN
08 09 10 11 12 13 14   10 9 8 7 6 5 4 3 2 1
First Edition

Dear Parents,

What Do You Need? books are a great way to get children interested in reading while encouraging them to use their imaginations. It is our hope that the What Do You Need? books will inspire life-long passions for reading and spark delightful interactions between you and your children. Discuss the title of this book with them and see what they have to say. You'll be surprised!

Enjoy our story,

Blaze and Maddy❀

"Any parent who reads to their children and participates in their child's development needs to ask themselves, 'What do you need…'"
—Nathan Jorgenson, award-winning author

"WDYN Books—what a delightful way to encourage children to read and challenge their inquisitive young minds."
—Mary Hiniker, reading specialist, Hudson School District, Hudson, WI

"Kids will love this imagination-sparking book!" —Ted Hustead, Wall Drug

"Hey, Maddy, wake up!"

"Why, Blaze? What's going on?"

"Dad's taking us camping
in the forest!"

WHAT DO YOU NEED?®

"Wow! That sounds like fun, Blaze."

"Let's hurry and get our stuff ready."

"But Blaze, I've never gone camping before.
I don't know what to take!"

"I told Dad the same thing, Maddy,
and he said we're both smart kids
and that we'd figure it out."

"We *are* smart kids, Blaze.
We *can* figure it out. Let's start packing!"

"Bunkbeds! We'll feel right
at home with these."

"And with the stove
we can make hot chocolate."

WHAT DO YOU NEED?®

"Clothes! We'll need lots of clothes!
Clothes for when it's cold
and clothes for when it's hot."

WHAT DO YOU NEED?®

"Let's see, we have our beds,
clothes, and something for cooking."

"What else do we need, Maddy?"

"Toast! I love toast! I'm going to bring the toaster!"

"Good idea, Maddy. I'm bringing the TV
so we won't miss any of our favorite shows."

"Books! I never leave home without books!"

"Oh boy, Blaze, we sure have a lot of books! You'd better get something to put them in."

WHAT DO YOU NEED?®

"Good idea! Here's the grandfather
clock from the dining room."

"Hey, Maddy! I almost forgot!
We need something to keep our food cold!"

"Relax, Blaze! I already
have it under control."

"We practice playing the piano every day.
We'd better bring it along, too."

"Okay, Blaze . . . I mean, NO!"

"Why not, Maddy? We have to practice."

"No, no, no! I don't mean that,
Blaze. Look at our pile of stuff!"

"Wow! It's a big pile."

"Yeah, Blaze, a big pile of all the wrong stuff."

"It sure is. I don't think
we could squeeze
all of those clothes
into our backpacks."

WHAT DO YOU NEED?®

"And no matter how hard we try, the piano
and bunkbeds are not going to fit into the car."

"Hey, Maddy, maybe we should ask Dad
what we really need to go camping."

"I think Dad would want us
to try to figure it out ourselves."

"Yeah, you're right about that."

"It's great to play the piano, Blaze,
but we won't need it in the forest."

WHAT DO YOU NEED?®

"Yeah Maddy, I think that goes for the stove, too. Dad can make a fire so we can cook our food. After all, he is a fireman!"

20

"What were we thinking, Blaze? There isn't any electricity in the forest. We'd better put the TV, toaster, and refrigerator back where they belong."

"You're right Maddy. Let's go find some real camping gear."

"It's going to be beautiful weather, so we won't need to bring all of our coats and sweaters."

"But we should each bring a rain jacket in case it rains."

WHAT DO YOU NEED?®

"Why don't we each pack one book in our backpacks along with our clothes?"

"That's a great idea, Maddy!

"Let's show Dad what we have so far
and see if he has any other ideas."

"Yeah, Blaze! Maybe *he* will
want to take the piano!"

WHAT DO YOU NEED?®

Two Harbors, MN
33 miles

Prescott, WI
232 miles

Jackson, MN
374 miles

Wall Drug
765 miles

Over There 1 mile

Under There
1/2 mile

Under Where?
0 miles

MAP

HAPPY
CAMPING!

WHAT DO YOU NEED?®

LOOK AND FIND

What camping items can you find in this picture? Can you find the small toy piano hidden in the pile? Can you think of anything else you might need to take camping that's not in this picture? Blaze and Maddy forgot to pack some bug spray. Look back through the book and see if you can find it.